JOHN
ELWAY

JOHN
ELWAY

BOB TEMPLE

THE CHILD'S WORLD®, INC.

ON THE COVER...

Front cover: John smiles as he jokes with his teammates during training camp on July 28, 1998.
Page 2: John holds the Super Bowl trophy after the Broncos win over the Green Bay Packers on January 25, 1997.

Library of Congress Cataloging-in-Publication Data
Temple, Bob.
John Elway / by Bob Temple.
p.   cm.
Includes index.
Summary: A brief biography of the quarterback who led the
Denver Broncos to two consecutive Super Bowl victories.
ISBN 1-56766-661-2 (library reinforced : alk paper)
1. Elway, John, 1960– Juvenile literature.
2. Football players—United States Biography Juvenile Literature.
3. Denver Broncos (Football team) Juvenile Literature.
[1. Elway, John, 1960– . 2. Football players.]   I. Title.
GV939.E48T46   1999
796.332'092—dc21   99-12988
[B]   CIP
                           AC

PHOTO CREDITS

All photos © AP/Wide World Photos

TABLE OF CONTENTS

CHAPTER   PAGE

On Top of the World 7

A Coach's Son...7

A Great Athlete 8

A Two-Sport Star 11

Getting Started 12

"The Drive"...14

Super Bowl Years..17

Terrell Davis Helps Out 18

Finally, a Dream Comes True 18

Twice Is Nice 21

The End of the Road 21

Timeline 23

Index & Glossary 24

ON TOP OF THE WORLD

John Elway stood on the podium holding the **Super Bowl** championship trophy. His Denver Broncos team had just won the Super Bowl for the second year in a row. This game was John's fifth Super Bowl, and it was also his best. His completed a long pass for a **touchdown** and even ran in a touchdown himself. Because he had played so well, John was named the Most Valuable Player of the Super Bowl.

A COACH'S SON

John Elway was born on June 28, 1960, in Port Angeles, Washington. John has a twin sister, Jana. John's dad, Jack Elway, was a football coach. He helped John learn about the game and made sure John had the best coaches available.

← John lifts the Super Bowl trophy after the Denver Broncos beat the Atlanta Falcons on January 31, 1999.

A GREAT ATHLETE

John Elway has always been a great athlete. As a boy, he was a great baseball player and football player. Even when he was just a preschooler, John could bat both left-handed and right-handed. And no one had to teach him how!

In football, John's position is **quarterback.** The quarterback is in charge of a football team's **offense.** It is his job to try to help his team score as many points as possible. A quarterback also has to have a strong arm, so he can make good passes to his receivers. John has one of the strongest arms of any quarterback ever to play the game. In some games, he has thrown the ball about 70 yards in the air!

John has always been a fast runner, too. In elementary school, John was the fastest boy in his class, so he always played running back on the football team.

John scrambles during the first half of the Super Bowl on January 25, 1998.

→

A TWO-SPORT STAR

In high school, John was an outstanding athlete in both football and baseball. His family had moved to California, and John attended Granada Hills High School. When John was a senior, he led the baseball team to the Los Angeles City Championship, batting .491 during the season. In football, he was named to four different all-America teams.

Because of his talents, many colleges were **recruiting** John to play football for them. Then in 1979, he was **drafted** by the Kansas City Royals of Major League Baseball. John had to make a decision: Did he want to play college football or professional baseball?

John was also an excellent student, so he chose to play college football at Stanford University in Palo Alto, California. While he was in college, John set lots of football records. He was an all-American again, and finished second in the voting for the Heisman trophy in his senior year. He set all sorts of new records at Stanford and broke five major national records, too.

A senior at Stanford, John throws a pass during the East-West Shrine game in 1983.

In 1981, John was again selected in the baseball draft, this time by the New York Yankees. He played for the Yankees' minor-league team in Oneonta, New York, in 1982. John liked playing professional baseball, but his real dream was to play in the National Football League. In 1983, the Baltimore Colts had the first pick in the NFL draft, but John didn't want to play for them. He asked them to trade their pick to a different team, because John wanted to play for a team on the West Coast. The Colts went ahead and drafted him anyway, and John said he would not play for them. He didn't think it was fair that he didn't get to decide where he got to play. Eventually, the Colts traded him to the Denver Broncos, and John was happy.

GETTING STARTED

The Broncos were the perfect team for John. They liked to pass the ball a lot, and John was definitely good at that. John soon earned a reputation for his strong arm, his quick feet, and his ability to rally his team when it was behind. In just his first three seasons, John proved he could be a winning quarterback. He was racking up the passing yards and leading NFL quarterbacks in rushing yards almost every year.

At this news conference in 1983, John tells reporters that he will play baseball for the New York Yankees.

→

"THE DRIVE"

Most people believed that John was ready to become one of the greatest quarterbacks in the NFL. But John hadn't taken his team to the Super Bowl yet. After the 1986 season, John took the Broncos to the AFC Championship Game against the Cleveland Browns. They were one win away from the Super Bowl.

With a little more than five minutes left to play, the Broncos were losing 20-13. To make matters worse, the Broncos were on their own two-yard line—98 yards away from a touchdown. If there was one thing that John always believed, it was that he shouldn't give up until time had run out.

John moved the Broncos swiftly down the field as the clock ticked down. Finally, with only 39 seconds left in the game, John threw a touchdown pass to Mark Jackson to tie the score at 20-20. In overtime, John drove the Broncos 60 yards to get them in position to kick the game-winning field goal.

John had done it. He had proven that he was one of the top quarterbacks in the NFL. That 98-yard **drive** cemented his place in Denver history and is considered one of the best drives in the history of the NFL. It will always mark John's career. In Denver, when someone says, "The Drive," people know they are referring to John's 98-yard drive in the AFC Championship Game.

John prepares to throw the ball during the 1987 AFC championship game against the Cleveland Browns.

SUPER BOWL YEARS

Early in his career, John took the Broncos to the Super Bowl three times in four years. They made it to the Super Bowl after the 1986, 1987 and 1989 seasons—but they did not win any of them.

John was starting to worry that he would never win "The Big One." He was always considered to be among the best quarterbacks in NFL history. As the years went by, John continued to shine. He set numerous records and brought the Broncos from behind many times. He was named the NFL's Most Valuable Player in 1987, made many trips to the Pro Bowl, and was clearly headed for the Hall of Fame.

But without a Super Bowl victory, John felt his career wasn't complete. Why couldn't the Broncos do it? One problem was that they relied on John too much. He was such a great quarterback that the Broncos didn't concentrate on running the ball. They wanted John to win every game with his passing. He often did—he brought the Broncos from behind in the fourth quarter 47 times in his career.

John throws a pass before a player for the San Francisco 49ers grabs him during a game in 1990.

TERRELL DAVIS HELPS OUT

In 1996, the Broncos began to rely on the running of Terrell Davis to help out the offense. They found that when Terrell had a good game running, it made it easier for John to pass the ball, too. That year, the Broncos had the best record in the NFL. This time, surely they were ready to win the big game. However, in their first playoff game, the Broncos were upset by the Jacksonville Jaguars. It was a very difficult loss for the Denver players to take.

FINALLY, A DREAM COMES TRUE

After the 1997 season, John finally got what he always wanted. He led the Broncos to the Super Bowl for the fourth time in his career. This time, they defeated the Green Bay Packers to win the championship. John didn't have his best game, but he inspired his teammates to do great things. Many players said they wanted to win the game for John, because they knew how important it was to him. After the game was over, Broncos owner Pat Bowlen held up the trophy and said, "This one's for John."

John celebrates on the shoulders of his teammates after the Broncos' first Super Bowl win in 1998.

→

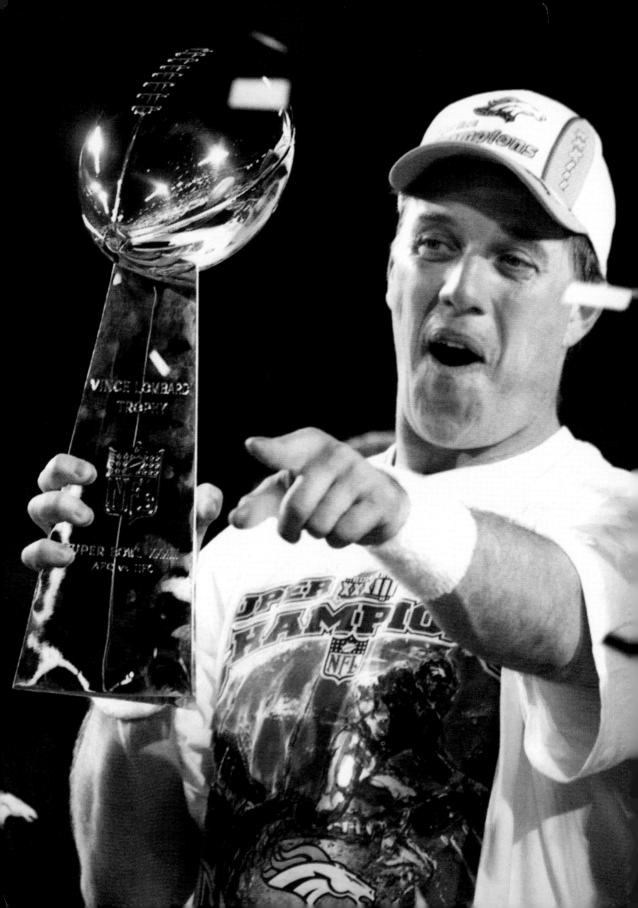

TWICE IS NICE

After the Super Bowl, John thought about retiring from football. In his years of playing the game, John had suffered many injuries. His body was sore, and he wasn't sure if he could handle another season of getting tackled by 300-pound men.

But John decided to come back, and he was up to his old tricks. He became just the second player to pass for more than 50,000 yards in a career. He also reached 300 career touchdown passes and became the only quarterback to start in the Super Bowl five times. This time, the Broncos defeated the Atlanta Falcons. A year after the team won the big game for John, he said, "This one's for the fans."

THE END OF THE ROAD

After winning his second straight Super Bowl, John realized that he had accomplished everything he dreamed of accomplishing. His injured knees were aching, and he decided it was time to retire. On May 2, 1999, John held a press conference to let everyone know he was not coming back for another season. The NFL will miss John's exciting plays, and it won't be long before he is included in the Hall of Fame.

John celebrates as he holds the Bronco's second Super Bowl trophy on January 31, 1999.

June 28, 1960	John Elway is born in Port Angeles, Washington.
1979	John leads his high school baseball team to the Los Angeles City championship. He is drafted by the Kansas City Royals of Major League Baseball. He is named to four different all-America teams in football. He signs a letter of intent to attend Stanford University and play college football.
1979-82	John sets five major Division 1A records and nine major Pac-10 records. He sets almost every Stanford career passing record.
1983	John is selected by the Baltimore Colts as the first overall pick in the NFL draft. He is soon traded to the Denver Broncos.
January 1987	John takes the Broncos to the Super Bowl for the first time in his career. He engineers the game-tying drive against Cleveland, a drive that marks him as perhaps the best fourth-quarter quarterback in NFL history.
1987	John is named the NFL's Most Valuable Player.
January 1988	John takes the Broncos to the Super Bowl for the second year in a row.
January 1990	John leads the Broncos to the Super Bowl for the third time in four years.
1996	John leads Broncos to the best regular-season record in the NFL, but they lose in their first playoff game.
January 1998	John leads the Broncos to their first Super Bowl victory.
January 1999	John leads the Broncos to their second straight Super Bowl victory and wins the Most Valuable Player award in the game.

John holds his award for Most Valuable Player while he stands next to Bronco's head coach Mike Shanahan.

GLOSSARY

drafted (DRAF–ted)
When athletes are drafted, they are picked to play on a professional team. John Elway was drafted with the first overall pick by the Baltimore Colts in 1983.

drive (DRYV)
When a football team uses many plays to move the ball toward the other team's end zone, it is called a drive. John Elway led the Broncos on a 98-yard drive to help them win the 1986 AFC Championship Game.

offense (AW–fents)
In football, the team that has the ball and is trying to score is on offense. John Elway plays on offense for the Broncos.

quarterback (KWOR–ter–bak)
The player in charge of the offense is the quarterback. John Elway is considered one of the best quarterbacks ever.

recruiting (ree–KROO–ting)
When colleges attempt to convince high school athletes to come to their school, it is called recruiting. Many colleges were recruiting John Elway when he was in high school.

Super Bowl (SOO–per BOHL)
The championship game in the National Football League is called the Super Bowl. John Elway has started in five Super Bowls, more than any other quarterback.

touchdown (TUTCH–down)
When a player carries the football into the other team's end zone, it is called a touchdown. John Elway passed for more than 300 touchdowns in his career.

INDEX

all-America teams, 11
Atlanta Falcons, 21
Baltimore Colts, 12
baseball, 8, 11, 12
birthday, 7
Bowlen, Pat, 18
Cleveland Browns, 14
Davis, Terrell, 18
Denver Broncos,
    7, 12, 14, 17, 18
draft, 12
drafted, 11
drive, 14
family, 7, 11
Green Bay Packers, 18
growing up, 8
Hall of Fame, 17, 21
Heisman trophy, 11
high school, 11
injuries, 21
Jacksonville Jaguars, 18
Kansas City Royals, 11
Los Angeles City
    Championship, 11
Major League Baseball, 11
Most Valuable Player, 17
National Football League,
    12, 14, 17, 18
New York Yankees, 12
offense, 8, 18
Pro Bowl, 17
quarterback, 8, 12, 14
records, 11, 21
recruiting, 11
retiring, 21
Stanford University, 11
Super Bowl, 7, 14, 17, 18, 21
timeline, 23
touchdown 7